Neeka and the Daylight Savings Bank

Akmed Khalifa

Illustrations
Nicole Osinde

ISBN 978-0-578-24793-9

Dedication

To my three children

Traci, Herman, and Frank, and my nephew Mike who has always seemed like one of my children

Acknowledgments

Tamica Tody

The musicality of her name inspired the naming of Neeka. I also imagined Tamica gracefully dancing around bees.

Frank Khalifa

My youngest son's first name inspired the naming of Neeka's friend Tank. I also recalled him as a very young boy playfully stomping his feet in the backyard, shooing birds from the trees.

The Pittsburgh Foundation

Funding for this publication was provided by the Advancing Black Arts in Pittsburgh Fund of The Pittsburgh Foundation

Illustration Credits

There was a girl named Neeka
Who loved to run in high top sneakas
She climbed tall trees
Danced around bees
And wanted to become a teacher

She was very smart
But afraid of the dark
Had ideas in her head
Monsters under her bed
Came from a tree in the park

While walking her dog with Dad
She talked about dreams she had
That a witch flies into her room
And under her bed on a broom
And makes the monsters mad

Why she asked does it get dark
And why does my dog never bark
Why is there daylight savings time
And is someone keeping mine
At a savings bank in the park

No daylight savings bank Dad said
That's just an idea in your head
So many questions my dear
There are no witches to fear
And no monsters under your bed

But Dad I hear monsters at night
That give me a terrible fright
If I had daylight on my door
I could sprinkle it on the floor
And run them out of sight

Neeka wanted to find that bank
But she needed help from Tank
Who lived across the street
Made birds fly by stomping his feet
And had a cat that never drank

So very early one morning
Before the birds could sing
Neeka, her dog, and Tank
With his cat that never drank
Left as the sun was rising

They walked up a little hill
And past a wagon wheel
Down by a playground
They walked out of town
And near a little windmill

Down a narrow road
Through a tall meadow
Across a little stream
Over an old wood beam
And past a croaking toad

Then came a river wide
That rushed and dived
And rolled and tossed
But needed to be crossed
Over to the other side

They all jumped in
And tried to swim
The current was fast
Each stroke could be last
Things were looking dim

They all might just drown
While bobbing up and down
Then Tank's cat took a gulp
And swallowed the river up
They were back on solid ground

Sitting on the riverbank
That fat cat of Tank's
Opened up his mouth
And let the water out
That he quickly drank

Then they walked to a tree
Its end they couldn't see
Neeka reached the top
Before she had to stop
And pushed aside the leaves

Then before her eyes
Stood a big surprise
A street to walk upon
That wasn't very long
Beneath the morning sky

Neeka took a chance
Climbed out on a branch
Pushed off with her feet
Landed on the street
And did a happy dance

At the end of the block
Beneath a giant clock
Was a building with a sign
That said that it saved time
Then Neeka began to walk

The building big and bright
Was open day and night
Neeka neared the door
Walked over the marble floor
And asked to buy some light

She took from her pocket
A red and yellow locket
That she had made
But was willing to trade
And then the banker bought it

Neeka told them thanks
For light for her and Tank
As she ran across the floor
Through the open door
And away from the bank

But something was wrong
It was taking far too long
To find the right tree
She just couldn't see
The wind was blowing strong

Tree tops were full of birds
She yelled but no one heard
That is except her dog
Who jumped upon a log
And barked his only word

Tank from across the street
Stomped and stomped his feet
Then birds flew from trees
Neeka could finally see
And grabbed a branch and leaped

She climbed down and down
Until she reached the ground
She handed Tank a bag of light
Then they ran to beat the night
And rode the river on a raft they found

Home at last they said goodbye
Neeka turned and ran inside
She hugged Mom and then Dad
Ran to her room with her bag
To get ready for the night

She hung it on her door
To use it later on the floor
Then jumped into her bed
And on her pillow laid her head
To wait for nighttime visitors

Soon Neeka nodded off to sleep
Into her room monsters creeped
And under where she laid her head
A mean green witch flew under the bed
Then Neeka jumped onto her feet

Took some daylight from the door
And threw a handful on the floor
Witches and monsters then took flight
To escape the bright daylight
Only to return no more

Now everything seems just right
Neeka has sweet dreams at night
Since her trip with friend Tank
To the Daylight Savings Bank
Sleep tight baby girl sleep tight

About The Author

Akmed Khalifa was born and raised in Pittsburgh, Pennsylvania, and grew up in Homewood's African American community. Akmed is an educator, poet, author, and playwright. He is also a retired adjunct professor and has earned three college degrees, including an MLS and an MFA, and spent a year as an artist in residence at The Minneapolis Playwright's Center. This is the sixth book that he has authored.

About The Illustrator

Nicole Osinde is a young African American artist who exhibited her considerable artistic talent early in life and, as a ninth-grade student, illustrated Akmed Khalifa's first children's book (Lil' Spooney). She is currently a sophomore at the University of Minnesota, and the superb work offered in this book demonstrates that her talent and skill continue to grow exponentially.